Drowning in bad luck, Cari doesn't know where to turn when the unexpected happens. A loyal customer at her Key West café has left her an inheritance. She hopes for cash to save her restaurant but receives an old brass bottle that looks like a sex toy . . . and has Jez inside.

At six-four, he's built like a gladiator, has looks to die for, and oozes sexuality. He's also a jinn.

Color her enthralled and excited. Besides being one hot dude, he grants wishes, right?
Not for her. Ironclad tradition demands he serve men, not women. Of course, if she wants to get down and dirty with him, he'll gladly oblige.

Let the battle of the sexes begin. Before long, their differences fall away as they indulge in every lusty desire, while falling hard and fast. Ah, paradise. Until trouble arrives, threatening to pull them apart forever . . .

Well Endowed
Copyright © 2019 Tina Donahue
ISBN: 978-1-4874-2609-5
Cover art by Martine Jardin

Published by eXtasy Books Inc or
Devine Destinies, an imprint of eXtasy Books Inc

Look for us online at:
www.eXtasybooks.com or www.devinedestinies.com

Well Endowed

By

Tina Donahue

CHAPTER ONE

The last place Cari Rayes wanted to be was outside a freaking attorney's building. A Mr. Antonini, according to his cryptic voicemail that told her squat. He didn't even have an online listing. What lawyer failed to do so and didn't advertise on TV or bus stop benches?

Unless he had something to hide. His name did sound like someone who buried secrets for the mob, or planned to sue her into everlasting poverty.

Please, not that. She was only twenty-six and already felt older than dirt.

Something plopped on her head.

Chin raised, she faced the churning clouds. A sudden downpour hit her. "Damn."

The weathercaster had claimed Key West would suffer no more than a brief sprinkle today before the summer sun and a caressing breeze returned. Wind lashed her and sodden hair clung to her neck. Her damp top proved ideal for a wet T-shirt contest, while stains dotted her bib apron from cooking for patrons at her café.

She hadn't thought to change before coming here from work. She couldn't think period, her worry stuck on Antonini killing her business and possibly making her homeless.

Bile rose in her throat. At this point, pretending he hadn't phoned was her best option, fleeing her second choice.

Her heart raced, but her legs wouldn't work. *Come on, dammit, move.*

Tap, tap, tap.

The noise came from a side window an elderly woman jabbed her forefinger against. She glared at Cari over half-lens reading glasses then impatiently gestured her inside the building. Given the late hour and the Wicked Witch's pursed lips, she appeared to work here and was eager to leave.

Too damn bad. Cari plodded inside at a slothlike pace, leaving damp shoeprints on the hardwood floor.

The Witch made a face. "Ms. Ryan?"

"No." Maybe this was a mistake. "Rayes."

She frowned at her computer screen. "So it is. In there." She gestured to an imposing door.

It didn't look inviting enough to open. Nausea rolled through Cari. "I know what this is about, and it took me by surprise. I didn't expect—"

"Yes, yes, yes. Don't keep Mr. Antonini waiting. He'll explain everything."

Precisely what she feared. Once she had a death grip on the knob, she pushed against the door. It creaked like the entrance to Dracula's tomb.

Inside the dimly lit space, countless books rose from floor to ceiling. A musty smell permeated, something akin to wet dog odor.

She wrinkled her nose and breathed through her mouth.

A gnome-like man sat behind a massive desk, his bald head not quite reaching the top of his huge leather chair. He looked up from his computer screen, its light reflected on his glasses. "Ms. Rayes?"

Her stomach dropped. She'd hoped he'd get her name wrong and she could flee. "Yeah. Look, I know what this is about." She closed the door and hurried to his desk. "My payments aren't that late. Only a week. Okay, two. I should have the cash tomorrow. At the most, by the weekend. He embezzled the money. I sure as hell didn't. It's my business. Why would I—"

"Embezzled?" Mr. Antonini sat straighter, adding an extra inch to his meager height. "There's been a crime? Do the police know?"

Not a chance. She hadn't wanted to face their pointed questions and condescending judgment as to what a fool she'd been, followed by her wait for them to get her dough back, which they wouldn't. The money was long gone, along with her hope. Despite the dank air in here, heat stung her face and throat. "Ah, it happened recently. When Matt didn't show up for work that Monday, I thought he'd slept in. No biggie. Everyone needs extra rest. But—"

"Matt?"

Shame gripped her. "My former boyfriend. We dated like forever." Tears pricked her eyes. "I believed he cared for me. That's why I let him move into my place and handle the café's books. He has an accounting degree and he—"

"I'm sorry to hear that. Not the degree part, the other matter. However, this meeting concerns Mrs. Kremp."

The name didn't register. "Is she the person who owns my apartment building or where I have my café?"

"I don't believe so." He checked his computer screen, scrolled for a second, then shook his head. "There isn't a commercial building or apartments listed in her assets. A shame. They would have made good investments." He leaned back. "I regret to inform you she passed early last week."

"How awful. But what does that have to do with me?"

"According to information I have, she frequented your café several times each week. Some might say she was your best customer."

Cari's legs gave out. She plopped into a leather chair facing the desk. "You're talking about Ethyl?"

"Yes."

A sweet old lady who loved Cuban fare and couldn't wolf down buñuelos, croquetas, fritas, arroz con pollo, and ropa vieja fast enough despite her frail build and deathly pallor. "Are you implying my cooking killed her?"

His eyes widened, then narrowed. "I doubt the sodium and cholesterol did her any good, but no. She was free to eat as she wanted and apparently enjoyed it so much she put you in her will."

Floored, she couldn't stop shaking. "Seriously? Just because she liked my cooking?"

"And how nice you were for taking a few minutes to speak to her each time she came in."

Ethyl had reminded Cari of her abuela — grandmother. She and Cari's grandfather had emigrated from Cuba and established the café, a Key West staple. When they passed, she'd taken over their beloved restaurant, promising to keep it alive, and would have retired most of their debt if Matt hadn't robbed her blind. "She was sweet. I liked her."

"And she liked you. Let's get to your inheritance."

Perspiration rolled down Cari's back, from excitement this time rather than fear. Even if Ethyl had only left her a few hundred bucks, the cash would help. If it were thousands or millions . . .

Suppressing a squeal, she rocked in place.

He swiveled in his chair, grabbed a dishtowel off the credenza behind him, and wrapped his hands in the cloth.

What in the fuck is he doing?

She craned her neck. No good. The chair hid his movements.

He turned back, holding a brass bottle, the towel protecting the surface.

Didn't make sense. The ancient metal had seen better days, its shine long gone, several nicks and dents marring it further.

He set it on the desk, then gingerly pushed it toward her.

The top had a knoblike shape tapering to a thick, yet long column. The bottom flared into two parts, similar in appearance to ripe peaches. Her heart sank. "She left me a brass dildo?"

"What?" He lifted his glasses and squinted, taking the bottle in. "It does look like one, doesn't it? I'd never noticed. But no, it's not, uh, what you called it." His glasses fell back to his nose. "Go on. It's yours." He eased it closer, his hands still wrapped in the towel.

She leaned away. "Is it a priceless antique?"

"More than you can imagine. However . . ." He dropped the towel, rapped his desk, and gave her a stern look. "You are not to sell it *ever*, no matter how desperate you are for money. If you even tried, well, I'd rather not go into what could happen."

Given how much she loathed bad news, she should have dropped the subject, but couldn't. "You're threatening to do what? Sue me? Kill—"

"No, no, no." He waved his hands. "Let's just say selling the item is ill advised. The contents aren't for sale either."

She finally got it, sort of. "Ethyl's ashes are in there? This is her urn?"

He laughed, choked, then coughed vigorously, his complexion changing from gray to bright red. "Excuse me." He cleared his throat. "Mrs. Kremp is buried in a very nice cemetery. I nearly forgot." He rifled through folders on his desk, pulled out a photo, and offered it to her. "She wanted you to have this."

The picture showed Ethyl lying in a coffin, a smile on her face, her gray hair done up the way she liked.

"Go on." He shook the photo. "Take it."

She bit her lip, but accepted the picture then tapped the corner. "This is autographed." Holy hell, her name was scrawled on it. "How is that possible?" She flung the photo on his desk. "She didn't come back from the dead to sign it, did she?"

"Of course not. She had the shot taken weeks before she

passed, wanting to make certain she looked good on her big day."

Big what? "She told you that?"

"And everything else. I've been her family's retainer for years. You should keep this memento." He touched the photo. "She wanted you to have it, along with the bottle."

He glanced at the container furtively, as one would plutonium or explosives.

"What's in the bottle? Was there a Mr. Kremp? Are his ashes in there?"

"No." Antonini straightened his folders. "She disposed of his at a landfill, shortly after leaving the crematorium." He looked up. "Their marriage had challenges."

Clearly. "I'm sorry to hear it. How about we open this baby now and see what's inside."

"*No.*" He jumped from his chair and held out his hands, stopping her from touching the bottle. "The will stipulates you cannot open the container until you're alone. By that, I mean completely. Do not take the top off while you're at work, on the bus, walking on the street, or wherever there are other people. Is that clear?"

"Not even close." She pushed to her feet. "Is there contraband in there? Will it get me arrested?"

He looked down his nose at her, which wasn't easy given she was inches taller. "What's inside isn't anything law enforcement cares about, but it is priceless and yours to do with as you will. No one — least of all me — will stop you."

She couldn't sell the bottle or the contents but doing what she wanted with them was fair game? Didn't make sense, unless . . . Visions starring precious jewels and gold coins danced in her head. Enough wealth to use as collateral to save her café from what Matt had done. She wanted to throw her arms around Antonini and kiss his wrinkled cheek but resisted. Dust or dandruff speckled the shoulders on his jacket.

Ew. "Thanks."

He nodded and gestured her away from his desk. "You can leave now."

"I don't have to sign anything?"

"No. Just take the bottle." He pressed a button on his phone and leaned down to it. "You can close up."

"She's leaving?"

"Yes."

"Thank God."

Before they threw her on the street, Cari lifted the bottle, surprised and pleased at how heavy it was. The contents had to be gold, possibly humongous diamonds, too. Excited, she eased the container into her oversized purse. "Bye."

Antonini stepped back, putting distance between them.

The Wicked Witch held the front door open despite rain and wind sweeping in.

Once Cari stood outside getting drenched, the door slammed behind her. A metal click sounded. The lock thrown.

Odd behavior even for the strangest people she'd ever met. Disquiet pressed close, making her stomach churn. On its heels, memories of Ethyl's sweet face and gentle laughter returned, then how the older woman always held Cari's hand as they spoke, her loneliness obvious.

Tears stung her eyes. No way would Ethyl do anything mean or hurtful. She'd provided an out, and no matter what, Cari would honor her memory as she did her grandparents'. Each week she'd place new flowers on Ethyl's gravesite, once she knew where it was. She'd make certain the cemetery workers tended the plot. She'd stop by as often as she could and have a chat, letting Ethyl know she wasn't alone or forgotten.

It was the least she could do.

Head bent against the driving torrent, she raced toward her apartment, several blocks away, curiosity and excitement building within her.

Once inside her snug kitchen, Cari flicked on the light to chase away the increasing gloom. Despite the dreary day, her apartment was still warm and fragrant from the buñuelos she'd made for breakfast, cinnamon and other spices scenting the air.

She placed her purse on the table, then used a fresh towel to dry her face, hair, and throat. Peeling off her soggy clothes seemed like a great idea, but anticipation kept her from it. She dropped her damp apron on a chair and reached inside her bag for the container.

Wait. Maybe there was a reason Antonini had held it in a dishrag. The bottle might be more fragile than it looked or felt.

With a towel in hand, she pulled the container from her purse, set it on the table, and frowned. There were odd symbols carved into the metal, not hieroglyphics, but images resembling penises and balls in every shape and size.

She curled her upper lip, not understanding why an old lady would have something like this, unless Ethyl's longings ran deeper than her love for Cuban fare or she'd liked to shop for smutty antiques.

Lightning flashed.

She flinched.

Thunder boomed.

So much for the promised nice weather, though the storm added a nice touch to her suspense as to the treasure awaiting her.

Given how much the bottle weighed, she predicted gold inside. However, if something clinked rather than rattled, that might mean jewels. She held the container to her ear and shook it.

Thunder cracked. A faint growl and clawing followed it.

What the?

Worried an animal was trying to dig its way inside her

place, she checked her windows. Nothing out there except flowers and bushes drowning in the rain.

Back at her table, she couldn't wait a second longer and twisted the knob to open the container.

The top didn't budge.

She tried repeatedly until she was breathless and sweating.

The fucking thing wouldn't turn. The nicks and dents she'd noticed earlier proved to be pry marks around the top that resembled the crown on a man's cock.

"Crap." She wasn't equipped to break this thing or saw it open.

After searching her kitchen for something to use, she settled on rubber gloves to add traction to her grip. With her thighs holding the bottle, she wrenched the top as hard as her strength allowed.

The knob not only loosened but flew off—similar to a cork on a champagne bottle—and hit her wall, denting the plaster.

There goes my security deposit.

Hold on.

By itself, the bottle trembled between her thighs, the metal growing warmer. Not an unpleasant feeling but fucking weird.

Appalled, she flung the container on her table.

It thudded dully against her purse and shook violently.

"Shit, shit, shit!" The damn thing was going to blow. Her spicy, rich cooking must have pushed Ethyl into an earlier grave than she wanted, and this was payback. Terrified, Cari dropped to her knees, desperate to crawl to the door and outside. Frozen in horror, she hunkered behind a chair for protection.

Thunder roared.

Gold-and-black smoke poured from the bottle.

I'm going to die.

Hard rain struck the windows, but they didn't blow out from an explosion.

Rather than the smoke rising to the ceiling, it curled in a slow spiral, then drifted away from the table to her side.

Shuddering, she crab-walked away from it.

The smoke followed and took form.

Feet appeared first, at least a size fifteen, the toes well-formed and long. Muscular calves and thighs materialized next, dark hairs hugging them, the complexion olive.

She stopped edging back and leaned forward instead.

Upper thighs and narrow hips emerged, a startling-white fabric tied around the groin area, the ends hiding the good stuff. Not a loincloth exactly, more like a scarf exposing a rock-hard ass.

The abs and chest were no different, each sculpted, the small nipples a dark brown shade, similar in color to refried beans. The pecs quivered on each new breath. However, there was no navel.

This can't be happening.

She raised her face.

The smoke broke apart, floated to the ceiling, and disappeared.

Leaving a thirtysomething man standing before her.

He opened his lushly lashed eyes.

Her breath caught. His irises were closer to gold than hazel, his shoulder-length brown hair thick and wavy, stubble outrageously sexy, mouth sensuous, one dark eyebrow arched at her.

He planted his hands on his lean hips.

Holy fuck. A gladiator couldn't have owned more muscles, though they weren't overdone like Arnold Schwarzenegger's, but totally male.

Her pussy creamed.

An odd reaction, since this couldn't be real.

When the knob flew off the bottle, it must have ricocheted off the wall and hit her head, causing her to hallucinate this, or rather, him.

Only one way to find out. She grabbed his calf. Its brawn and heat made her ears buzz.

Grinning lewdly, he flexed his muscles and pressed into her touch.

This was no dream. She snatched back her hand. "Who-who-who-who—" She shivered so badly she couldn't speak, but she had to. "Who are you? *What* are you?"

His eyebrows shot up to his hairline. He lifted his chin. "You, a mere woman, dare to question or demand anything from me?"

"Huh?" Not liking his sexist attitude, she scrambled to her feet. At five-seven, she couldn't match his height. By her guestimate, he topped out at six-four and was the most perfect man she'd ever seen, except for his patronizing gaze. Precisely what she didn't need. "Again, who or what are you? This is my place. My kitchen. Not yours. Answer me."

"I answer only to my master. Go on." He gestured her away as Antonini had. "Fetch the man in charge."

As if. Before she could slug him, he pivoted and regarded her kitchen warily, as a one-percenter would, seeing only how small and simple it was.

She couldn't have cared less if he found her digs lacking.

He next focused on her buñuelos.

If he gave them a pissy look or said one unkind thing about her cooking, he wasn't long for this world, even if she didn't know how to off him.

Bent at the waist, he sniffed the treats and licked his lips.

Growling sounded.

His stomach?

Holding one buñuelo between his thumb and forefinger, he examined the fried dough carefully, licked the contours, then popped the treat into his mouth. As he chewed, his lids slid down and he moaned the way guys did during orgasms.

The best compliment ever. Her folds grew damper and her

nipples peaked. "You like?"

Ignoring her question, he tongued sugar and cinnamon off his lips, then popped three more buñuelos into his mouth. "What do you call these?"

He could ask questions and expect answers, but she couldn't? She tapped her foot. "Mine."

He nodded, finished the rest, then cleaned his hands on the cloth hiding his family jewels. "Do you have more of the mine?"

She held back a snicker at his cluelessness. "Aw, are you hungry?"

"I could eat. Go on." He gestured to the kitchen in general. "Find me more mine. Bring them to me immediately as I await my master."

She grabbed a large wooden spoon to use as a potential weapon and tapped it against her leg. "Nothing's happening until you tell me who you are, or what you are, or both."

His jaw and shoulders tightened.

Oh please. When it came to the silent treatment, she could beat him, or any man, and kept her peace.

He shifted his weight, flexed his muscles, then huffed. "I'm a jinn." He jabbed his thumb at the dildo-shaped bottle. "Isn't that obvious?"

"Not to me. What's a jinn?"

Shock crossed his rugged features followed by condescension. "I know you're only a woman and not expected to know much, but you should at least—"

"Only. A. Woman? A *mere* woman?" She approached, her spoon pointed at the bulge between his legs, ready to castrate him. "Care to rephrase those comments?"

He stared at the spoon. "You're angry I ate your mine. I shouldn't have."

"That's right. You should have asked my permission first."

"Hunger made me weak." He hung his head.

She wasn't certain if he was putting her on or not. "You're made from smoke, but you eat and feel hunger pangs?"

"I can't explain it." He rubbed his growling stomach. "Or the sounds I make when my insides hurt for food."

Her caution fell away replaced by sympathy. "How long has it been since your last meal?"

"My Master's been gone for an eternity."

Antonini said Ethyl was buried last week. Maybe for a jinn that period was endless. "Have you ever had a mixto? It's a Cuban sandwich stuffed with ham, pork, salami, Swiss cheese, and pickles, then topped by mustard. I can make you one. Would you like to try it?"

His stomach rumbled. "How long would it be for you to make it?"

"A few minutes. You can have some croquetas while you wait."

"Are they like the mine?"

She stifled a smile, not wanting him to think she was having fun at his expense. "No. Croquetas have meat, fish, or vegetables in them. Give me a sec to heat them up."

"I can eat them cold."

He *was* hungry. "Sit." She pulled out a chair, put the mixto fixings on the table, then delivered the croquetas on a tray.

With the platter propped on one thigh, he rested his other foot on another chair.

Given his position, and how he wore his white cloth commando style, she had a ringside view of his balls and cock. Flaccid, his dick was easily eight inches, meaning ten or eleven inches when erect.

Her belly fluttered.

Short, dark hairs hugged his pendulous balls. An ancient and provocative fragrance scented him, far better than simple musk, something that brought to mind lusty nights, tangled limbs, an eager cock seeking a willing cunt, bodies, mouths, hearts, and souls joined.

Dizzy, she gripped the table for support.

He regarded her, crumbs dotting his lips. "Are you all right?"

Afraid to trust her voice, she nodded.

His gaze swept her. He lingered on her mouth, dropped to her hard nipples pressed against her wet tee, then focused on her fly.

His cock thickened and rose, pushing aside the cloth. "You smell good." His already deep voice had dropped several octaves. A faraway look glazed his eyes. "Are you hungry, too?"

If he was referring to sex, she hadn't been laid since Matt screwed her, figuratively and literally. He'd been no prize in bed or in the looks department. No biggie. She'd gravitated toward his emotional support and kindness, which was an act to suck her in.

Prick. She nodded.

He licked his fingers, tossed the empty platter toward the sink, and hauled her onto the table, placing her flat on her back.

Jeezus.

The tray clattered on the floor. She squirmed. "What are you doing?"

"Easing your hunger." He pressed his mouth to her throat, his lips softer than a rose petal, his stubble rasping her, his breath heated and sweet. "And satisfying you."

She gurgled.

His mouth covered hers, his tongue plunging inside.

God, god, god. He tasted better than he looked, which didn't seem possible. His weight was a comfort rather than a burden, his warmth chasing away the worry she'd lived with too long. First, when her mother hadn't cared about her welfare, next when Mima and Pipo, her grandparents, had passed, then when she'd learned about the café's missing funds.

She gripped his hair, keeping him to her, and enjoyed him

as she had no other man.

As frantic as she behaved, he kept his pace lazy and sensual. His kiss explored rather than ravished.

Her nerve endings fired every-freaking-where. The needy woman she'd hidden from the world rose to the surface, wanting, craving a man's protective and commanding touch.

His tenderness evolved to raw lust, his desire insatiable.

No different from hers.

Their brutal kiss pressed her teeth into her inside lip, cutting it. She didn't care, wanting more.

He ripped off his cloth and dropped it next to her arm, then pushed her tee and bra up, exposing her breasts.

The rain had chilled them.

His lips warmed her flesh faster than she could blink. He sucked her nipples deeper into his hot, wet mouth.

Her scalp tingled. She panted.

Despite fumbling with her jeans' button and fly, he finally managed to free both, then eased his hand beneath them and her panties, straight to her drenched cleft, touching her clit.

Intense delight zipped from her cunt to points beyond. She bucked.

He grunted and held her down, enjoying her boobs while finger-fucking her with his thumb.

Pleasure curled inside her, then gathered in her pussy. A familiar heaviness settled there, accompanied by a pleasant ache.

As he stroked her nub relentlessly, he slipped two fingers into her sheath and spread them, preparing her for his mammoth cock.

Rapture filled her.

Alarm bells sounded in her head.

What in the fuck are you doing? He's not real. He's . . .

She hadn't a clue what he was and honestly didn't care but supposed she'd better before their depravity went too far.

Using all her strength, she shoved against his pecs.

He might as well have been stone.

Since she wasn't and would cave any minute to him licking her nipples and teasing her clit, she shouted, "Hey! Stop!" She kicked her legs.

His licking slowed, then halted. He lifted his face from her breast. "You came without me?"

For someone who lived in a bottle, he knew a lot about sex, yet didn't, given his question, which made zero sense. "How many women have you been with?"

His face colored. He grew uncharacteristically shy. "I'm no virgin."

"Sure about that? Your fingers are deep in my pussy. Do you feel contractions from my climax?"

"You might be different from any woman I've known."

If his great looks were any indication, he must have screwed with thousands. Not wanting to picture him having that much fun, or analyzing why his randy ways should bother her, she pushed against his chest.

He eased up and offered an imperious look. "How many men have you been with?"

"Too many, counting you. Wait. You're not a man. You're a jinn. What is that?" She grabbed her spoon from where it had landed on the table and shoved its farthest tip against his chest. "Answer me."

His impossibly broad shoulders tensed. "To your kind a jinn is known as a genie."

Considering he'd materialized from a brass bottle, she should have connected the dots on his answer before now, but shock had dulled her brain. No more. "Like in Aladdin?"

He stepped away from her, balls tight to his glorious bod, his cock jutting hard and proud from his hairy groin. "Must you insult me with your silly fables?"

"I didn't know I was." She pushed to her elbows. Her boobs wiggled.

16

He smiled.

Remembering her partial nudity, she pulled her bra and tee down, then fixed her panties and jeans. "What's the difference between a jinn and a genie?"

He stared at her covered boobs and gave her a sour look. "The same as between a majestic sunset and a child's finger painting."

Offense sounded in his voice, hurt beneath it. "Hey, I didn't mean anything by what I said. I've only read about genies—jinns—or seen them on TV, never in the flesh."

He scratched his ass, then his pit.

Dark hair peeked from it, masculine as fuck.

She trembled and couldn't focus on anything except his thickening cock. Ropy veins snaked over the hard column. The crown flushed maroon, proving his desire. Pre-cum beaded on the tiny slit.

Inch by inch, his dick lifted until it pointed at her cunt.

Her pussy clenched, wanting him inside. She fought the urge. "You should put your thing back on." She flung the cloth at him.

It hit his chest and fell to his cock, draping the shaft rather than dropping to the floor.

He was harder than steel. Warmth flooded her. With great effort, she concentrated on his face and tried to sound reasonable. "How is your kind possible?"

"Beats me." He gestured to the food strewn across the table, messed up by their gyrations. "Mind if I make that sandwich you mentioned?"

"A mixto. That's okay, I'll do it while we talk."

His features darkened.

Didn't matter. She needed to know details about her inheritance and hurriedly built the sandwich. "You served Ethyl?"

He shoved ham in his mouth and spoke around it. "Who?"

"Ethyl Kremp." She smeared yellow mustard on the

ciabatta bread. "Your Master. Or maybe it's Mistress when a woman's in command."

"That's not possible, and I did not serve her." He chewed and swallowed. "My masters have always been men. As it should be."

Ethyl couldn't haven't stolen the bottle from someone else. She was too nice. "Was your latest one named Kremp? Wait — what's your name? Do you have one?"

"Of course." Indignation flared in his eyes. "I'm Jezeed. Jez for short."

She liked it and smiled. "Cool name. I'm Cari. Nice to meet you, Jez." She put out her hand.

He brought her fingers to his mouth and sucked each one.

Her knees sagged and her head sank to the side.

Finished, he sniffed her palm, wrist, and arm. "You smell good. Like your mine I ate."

Uh-huh. She straightened. "Thanks. Maybe before my café goes bankrupt, I'll get into fragrances heavy on cinnamon and sugar. What do you mean you didn't serve Ethyl? When her husband passed, he must have left you to her. She was your new boss."

He crossed his arms over his chest and squeezed. Countless muscles bulged.

Her mouth watered.

"Are you going to call the man in charge in here or not? If not . . ." He eyed the bottle. "I'll return to my abode until he arrives."

"Yeah?" She advanced, crowding him to the point he should have stepped back. He didn't. Their feet and thighs touched. She wasn't one to mind, except for her heightened breathing giving away her arousal. Once she'd calmed herself, she laid down the law. "There is no man here. Just me. I'm the one in charge."

He shook his head. "Not possible. I only serve males. I

cannot — I *will not* — serve you."

If he hadn't looked so luscious and commanding, she would have kneed him in the balls. "What do you call what just happened on the table?" She swung her arm to it. "If that wasn't serving me, then what was it?"

He made a face. "Don't you know? Haven't you been with a man before?"

"Of course I have." She bounced on her heels. "As I was with you while you were serving my carnal needs."

His good mood returned. He gave her a sly look and leaned in. "So you were turned on."

Fuck. Talking to him was worse than what she'd experienced with other guys. "How did you serve Ethyl's husband, your last master?"

He tilted his face to the ceiling and breathed hard. "By granting wishes. That's what jinns do. You know, like Aladdin." He gave her a look.

She shot one right back. "What happened after his third and last wish? Did he wish for more on the final one?" Now was the time for particulars so she wouldn't fuck this up. If things worked out, she could save her café and get enough dough to buy her own house. She wouldn't be greedy, but would make sure she'd never be homeless or worried about money again. "Did he keep doing that so the wishes would continue?"

Jez rolled his eyes. "That's a silly myth."

"Okay. What happened after his third and last wish?"

"Nothing. The wishes are never ending. There is no limit. Only the master's death stops them."

Good frigging lord. She'd hit the jackpot.

CHAPTER TWO

Cari squealed, pumped her fists, and danced around the table, forgetting to finish Jez's sandwich.

For the moment, he didn't mind, entranced at how her boobs bounced.

Those babies had been a pleasant handful when she'd been on the table beneath him . . . where she belonged. No matter what she thought or said, it would always be a man's world. A woman's role was to make the stay nicer for the guy.

Had she ever for him.

His cock thickened from how achingly soft and strikingly warm her skin had been. No different from her narrow and wet pussy when he'd slipped two fingers inside.

A dazzling moment, the same as their kiss.

Heat rolled through him as he relived their lips touching, his tongue entering her mouth with a right he'd taken as a male. Along with what she'd allowed him.

He should have griped at granting her any power but smiled instead.

Despite the thousands of women he'd mounted during his endless existence, none had owned her sass, which he found intriguing and arousing. Other females had succumbed to his sexual prowess without hesitation. Not that he could blame them. He rocked in the sack. If they'd craved a wish, they'd tried seduction, not threats, to get him to do what they wanted.

His principles wouldn't allow it. He served men, not women. That was the way things were. As the saying went, *get over it already.*

She bounced in place, the numerous earrings she wore in each lobe swaying on every jump, her black hair sweeping over her shoulders, pretty face flushed.

His insides made a funny twist, part lust, part affection. He liked seeing her happy. Joy brought a deeper color to her tawny complexion. Her dark brown eyes sparkled, bliss registering in them. Her plush lips parted.

Winded at last, she joined him and held her fists to her outstanding chest, her nipples nearly as hard as his dick, her hips lush, legs long, scent fantastic, musk suffusing the food scents.

"Thank you!" She threw her arms around him and planted wet kisses on his cheek, chin, neck, collarbone . . .

Everywhere but the part he wanted.

Frustrated, he growled and lifted her into his arms.

She settled her legs around his hips and wreathed her arms over his shoulders, as she should.

He captured her mouth.

She thrust her tongue between his lips before he could do the same to her.

Desire slammed into him. He staggered.

She tightened her embrace.

Fine with him. He sucked her tongue forcefully.

Whimpers poured from her.

Nice. He squeezed her ass, liking the firm, plump cheeks. She was built as a woman should be — pure softness, no sharp angles, or anything hard. That was his department.

Panting, he slipped his hand beneath her jeans and panties to touch the silky furrow separating her butt cheeks. Upon reaching her anus, he stroked the tight ring.

She shivered and gripped his scalp, keeping him to her.

As if he'd be anywhere else.

Blindly, he lurched to the table, wanting her on it. If he'd known where her bedroom was, he would have sprinted there. For now, this would have to do.

He bumped into a chair. It skidded away. He reached the table and brought her down to it, away from his sandwich stuff.

She stiffened, then wiggled.

Starved for a full breath, he tore his mouth free, gulped air, and wheezed out his words. "Calm down. I'm moving as fast as I can. I'll have you naked in a sec." He grabbed her tee.

"Wait. Hold on."

"You want the jeans off first? Fine." If nothing else, he'd accommodate her in this. He shoved her to the table, yanked off her sneakers, and tossed them aside.

They hit the door.

She kicked her legs.

"Will you keep still?" He caught one leg and tore off her sock.

She pushed up and dug her nails into his wrists.

Fuck. "Ow." He bared his teeth. "What are you doing?"

"Getting you to hold on as I said." She released his left wrist and pushed hair off her face. "What do you think you're doing?"

He stated the obvious. "Bleeding. What else?"

She gaped at the lacerations she'd left on him. "You have blood?"

What did she think he had inside, rocket fuel? "Of course. Why so surprised?"

"You don't have a navel." She stroked his stomach.

The muscles quivered, the exquisite feelings she generated reaching his teeth and tongue. His mouth went so dry he had trouble speaking. "I wasn't born like you."

Sadness touched her eyes. She cradled his face, her thumbs stroking his cheeks. "How did you come to be?"

She wanted his history when his balls screamed for relief and his cock ached like a son-of-a-bitch? Any more pain and he'd sob worse than a little girl. "I don't know." He nuzzled her neck and swept his tongue over her velvety skin, enjoying its saltiness.

She sagged against him. "How far back do you remember?"

He shrugged and fooled with the button on her jeans.

"That far, huh?" Her breathy voice held an edge. She pushed his hand from her fly.

Damn. For the first time in forever, his carnal moves weren't cutting it. Time to try another approach. "Do you mind if we talk about this after we're through? I'm hurting here." He curled her fingers around his rigid dick.

Breath spilled from her. She stroked his length, circled the crown, then stopped.

Why? "Keep going." He forced down a swallow and used his most encouraging voice. "That feels great."

She jerked her hand away and scooted back on the table, away from him. "You're getting the wrong idea about me."

Her husky voice, heightened color, and heaving chest told him everything he needed to know. She was as horny as him. Despite that truth, he played her game. "I don't think so, since you're way over there and I'm way over here. Call me crazy, but there isn't a lot I can do if you keep running away." He pushed out his bottom lip. "Don't you like me?"

She snickered but sobered fast. "Finding you attractive has nothing to do with this." She smoothed her clothes. "I need to settle stuff about my wishes."

He backed away, his naked feet slapping her floor. "No. And that's final. I will not serve you or any female, *ever.*"

Her jaw tightened. She looked like she wanted to claw his eyes out.

He put additional space between them.

Her gaze noted his retreat and caution. Quickly, she calmed and tapped her chin. "You're sure about your decision not to grant me one puny wish? I mean totally certain, without any qualms whatsoever?"

He'd liked her better when she was pissed. Hysterics he knew how to deal with by simply ignoring them. Cold logic was something else. He was reluctant to ask what she meant, but she wasn't giving him another choice. "Why do you want to know?"

She stroked her bottom lip.

Its rosy color and fullness drew him like metal to a magnet. Without thinking, he edged closer, then stopped and locked his knees to keep put.

She regarded his cock.

Showing off, he flexed his dick until its head pointed at his other one, exposing and displaying his balls.

Approval shone in her eyes. A smile spread across her face.

He should have showed her this trick earlier. At last, she was crumbling to his male mastery, as she should. He stepped closer.

She made a purring sound, then met his gaze. "Easy, tiger, we haven't settled things yet."

They were back to that? "Fine. Settle them." He stuffed ham, salami, and pork into his mouth, then talked around the meaty wad. "Say what you have to say."

"I intend to." She jumped off the table but kept her distance. "If you refuse to grant me as much as one lousy wish, I'll have no choice but to put you back in the bottle and make sure you don't leave it. You dig what I'm saying? There won't be food in there like there is out here."

The meat stuck in his throat.

At his discomfort, a knowing look filled her face. "Ordinarily, I don't like to pull rank. I'm a reasonable person, but I am your Master or Mistress. Whichever title you prefer, though Cari will do. If I put you back in the bottle and you still refuse to serve me, I may have to throw you out, or give you to someone else."

That hurt. Already he liked her tiny place. It smelled wonderful, much better than the stale mansion his last master had lived in. A mausoleum was more enticing than that awful place.

He liked her, too, but wouldn't admit it. Showing weakness wasn't what males did, no matter the horror they faced. Standing his ground, he crossed his arms and met her stare for stare. "Do your worst."

Her mouth quivered, and her eyes got shiny.

Crap. He didn't want her to cry. Tears were his Kryptonite. He steeled himself against them.

Her breathing picked up. She made a snarling noise, her frustration and anger returning.

He couldn't have been happier.

She, on the other hand, was losing it. Brandishing her wooden spoon, she approached.

He talked fast. "There's no reason to get violent. If you want me back in the bottle, say so and I'm gone. However, I have a better solution."

She kept a reasonable distance from him and tapped her naked foot. "I'm listening."

He nodded. "I love your mine and everything else you cook. I'm sure you do, too. So let's spend our days eating your stuff and fucking. I know you like me." He wiggled his eyebrows. "You get all soft and sweet whenever my mouth and hands are on you. Just wait until my cock's inside your pussy, mouth, and what I like to call the back door. There will be no end to the good times. We can even do kink. Trust me, it's great." He caught a breath. "After we're through, I can sleep and recharge, while you cook more things — What are you doing?" He danced away from her and hit the wall.

She kept swinging her spoon at him. "If you think I'm going to sleep with you, and cook for you, *and* serve you, meaning I'm doing *all* the fucking work while you snooze, you have lost your goddamn mind." She threw the spoon.

It hit the wall to the side.

He didn't dare thank her for not braining him.

She tightened her fists to the point her knuckles blanched. "No guy will ever use me as Matt did. It's not happening. I'd see that prick dead first, understand?"

He bobbed his head in agreement. "Matt?"

"Never mind who he is." She paced. "I should put you in the bottle. Hell, I should throw you in the trash. Even better, I should give you to the Wicked Witch." She stopped and faced him. "That would be pure torture."

Sounded like it. "Who's the Wicked Witch?"

She strode past him, then around the table. "Unfortunately, I'm not that mean."

"I know. You're basically a nice person."

"Not that nice." She got in his face. "Beginning tomorrow, you're earning your keep here. You want to eat, you work first. You want to sleep, ditto what I've already said. You want to stay with me, you have to give me a reason to say yes."

He wasn't sure about hanging around any longer but wasn't going to argue. "As long as it doesn't involve wishes, I'll do whatever you want."

"You say that now." She pointed at him. "You have no idea what it takes to run a café, but you will. Believe it."

"Okay. Can I have my sandwich now?"

She bunched her shoulders, like a bull prepared to charge.

He tried to reason. "I did give you some dynamite kisses. Didn't I earn a bite of my sandwich for them?"

Her face changed, fury turning to hurt. "No, you did not. You should have kissed me because you wanted to. Because you couldn't help yourself." She stomped her foot. "Because you needed me more than anything else, even food or air."

Her passion surprised him, her feelings reaching deeper than mere lust. "Is that how you felt about me when we were enjoying ourselves?"

She turned her back to him and crossed her arms. "Clean up the mess you made in here. Put the food back in the refrigerator and wipe the table down. When what you've done meets my standards, you can return to your bottle to sleep. Better get a full eight hours, you have an early and long day tomorrow. By the way . . ." She looked over her shoulder at him. "Don't you dare use a wish to do what I just said. You'll finish the tasks the mortal way."

No kidding. "I can't use wishes for myself. It's not possible."

Surprise flicked across her features, then hardened to resolve. "Good. Now you'll know what I face every freaking day. Go on. Get started."

She treated him like his last master did his maids. Mr. Kremp had bossed them around endlessly, then fucked them silly even when his wife was around. Wasn't nice, but hey, Jez wasn't the purity police. He did as ordered. As a reward for his unwavering obedience, Kremp invited Jez to join him and the maids, each girl under twenty-five and eager to frolic with the boys. Those encounters were epic. When Kremp passed out after only one climax, Jez had the ladies to himself.

Cari cleared her throat. "What are you waiting for? Why are you smiling?"

He killed it, dragged himself to the table, and tossed food on the tray.

"Uh-uh. Everything in its rightful place, not in one heap."

Talk about being particular. He placed the coquetas where they should be, put his sandwich back together, and snuck a bite.

She pulled the food from him. "Have you earned this?"

"You mean your rude behavior?"

She chomped on the sandwich and licked mustard off her lips. "Go on. You're not close to being finished."

As she ate, he slaved, repeatedly retracing his steps when she complained about the way he folded the ham, stacked the pork, or licked mustard from the knife. Endless nitpicking. "What now?" He showed her the utensil. "You wanted it clean. It is."

"Not after you sucked on it. Put it in the sink with the other dishes. You'll do them once you clean the table."

He swore beneath his breath in English and his native tongue.

She swallowed her bite and cocked her head. "What was that?"

"My stomach's rumbling."

"I'll save you part of the sandwich. When you're through with your chores, you can have it."

At this rate, he'd starve.

What seemed hours later, he finished and sagged against the sink. "Anything else?"

Rather than answer, she pulled food from the fridge and placed it on the table.

He pointed at the trays. "I am not cleaning that up."

"No one asked you to." She built another mixto, this one twice as big as the first, and offered it to him on a plate. "See how nice I can be when you cooperate?"

He bit into the sandwich. *Whoa.* His taste buds came alive at the heavenly flavors. He moaned in appreciation. "Does this mean we'll screw after I'm finished?"

Her eyes went blurry and color stained her cheeks.

If that wasn't a yes, he didn't know what was. "I'll finish this baby in a flash. Just give me a sec."

"No." Her gaze cleared. She walked backward toward a doorway. "When you're through, put your dish in the sink and get whatever you want to drink from the fridge, then go

28

to bed."

The word gave him renewed hope. "With you?"

She frowned. "No. In your bottle. Or if you'd prefer, on the sofa in the living room." She jabbed her thumb toward the doorway. "It's to the right. My bedroom's in the opposite direction. Don't make a mistake and go there, understand?"

He didn't, not comprehending why she kept resisting him. "If that's what you want."

She rubbed her forehead. Her shoulders drooped. "It is." She pivoted and disappeared down the hall.

He called out, "Good night."

She didn't respond.

Curled in her bed, Cari struggled to relax and sleep, but couldn't.

Bottles and plates clattered in the kitchen. The table legs scraped the floor. A chair bounced, then made a gliding noise.

Jez was tearing her place apart and she didn't have the energy or will to stop him. Her bruised heart hurt too badly. First, Matt had used her, then Jez tried. If that wasn't bad enough, he'd believed kissing and having sex with her—in exchange for what he wanted—was all right. As though she was an ugly, old woman using him as her gigolo, because she had no other choice.

Damn him for making her doubt herself and touching her soul with his question about what she thought of him.

She liked him too much even though he got on her last nerve. What guy didn't? At least he was dumb as a rock when it came to interactions with modern women. She couldn't blame him for that if old man Kremp, and his other masters, had spouted sexist junk nonstop. It was all he knew.

She'd teach him better manners and would persuade him to grant her at least one wish. If she didn't, she'd lose her café and this place. They'd be out on the street. What a fucking mess that would be. Her homeless and taking care of a jinn who refused to grant her wishes.

Shit. She pulled her pillow over her head and prayed for unconsciousness.

More noise sounded from the kitchen. Him doing whatever as his ass clenched, dick swung, and balls plumped.

A pulse ticked deep within her pussy, hopeless arousal crowding out everything else.

Giving in, she stroked her clit.

Pleasure cascaded down her legs and up her stomach to her throat. Her mouth fell open.

Lonely and wanting, she fantasized about him doing her, his rigid cock piercing her soft folds, hands caressing her boobs, their mouths joined.

Intense heat roared through her. She stroked her clit faster and harder. Indescribable delight arrived in ever-increasing waves, tensing her inner thighs, and making the room spin.

She basked in satisfaction, drifted, and conked out.

A scream jarred her awake.

Jez.

Cari jumped from her bed and was halfway across the room when she realized her alarm was wailing away, the time 4:30 AM. Few appreciated how early cooks had to get to work for prep before the first patron strolled in the door.

Yawning, she padded to the kitchen and stopped dead.

Everything was in its place and gleaming, Jez nowhere in sight, his brass bottle on the stove.

She wasn't sure whether to tap it to wake him or if she should simply open the thing. She opted for the latter. Nothing happened, no smoke, shaking, or warmth. She peered inside.

Total darkness greeted her.

He couldn't have left.

Her heart cramped. She ran to the back door. Still locked.

Panicked, she bolted into the bath. Empty.

"Where the hell are you?" *Please, you have to be here.* Even if he never gave her a wish, she'd still miss him. "Jez!"

A snore rumbled in the living room.

Naked, he lay sprawled on the sofa, his hand on his limp dick, cum glistening on his thighs from his masturbation-fest. Having done the same, she couldn't blame him. The six-pack she'd bought was on the cocktail table, each bottle empty, but resting on coasters to avoid leaving rings.

The walls she built around herself crumbled. They shouldn't have, but she couldn't help her emotions. Tenderness welled in her at his thoughtfulness. Before she lost her good sense and threw herself at him, she shook his shoulder.

A snore caught in his throat. He coughed, opened one eye, and met her gaze.

An immediate smile touched his lips.

God, I want you. She sank to her knees and buried her face in his dark curls, reveling in his musky fragrance.

He sucked in a breath. His toes curled and splayed. "What are you doing?"

"This." She cradled his cock and licked it.

"*Why?*"

His panic surprised her. She lifted her face. "I'm giving you head." *What else?*

He gasped out his words. "You're not simply tasting my cock before chewing it off?"

A fair question given what a bitch she'd been the previous night. "Nope." She eased it aside and took his right ball into her mouth.

He shouted. "Yes, yes, yes! Don't stop!"

She hadn't planned to. This was as much for her as it was for him. She dragged her tongue across his nut, adoring its heat, saltiness, and rough hairs. Nothing could match a guy's balls for pure masculinity. There was something so damn decadent about them.

She shivered.

He writhed.

Taking care not to hurt him, she suckled his ball, breathed in his musk, and worked his cock in her palm as her pussy would.

He babbled a language she didn't understand. Not that comprehension mattered. Raw need and wonder rang in his voice, telling her he enjoyed what she did. His earlier smile proved he liked her.

She tended his other ball until he struggled to breathe. Not giving him a chance to recover, she took his cock into her mouth as deep as it could go, clear past her tonsils.

He gagged and bellowed.

A compliment on her delivery, and precisely the assurance she required. Men weren't the only ones who worried about performance. Women were equally fucked up.

With him, she sensed she didn't have to be. Desiring him came easy. Loving him like this was second nature.

She released his shaft from her mouth but pursed her lips around his crown, then drove him back inside while also fondling his balls.

He groaned. "I'm going to come! I can't hold off!"

She'd never ask him to do so. In this, his pleasure came before hers. She positioned his crown for the best access, then licked the bumpy skin in back.

He howled, beat his fists against the sofa, and came.

His thick, creamy cum spurted into her mouth.

She stilled. For him to have jizz suddenly hit her. He didn't have a navel, but could ejaculate?

What a mystery and marvel he'd turned out to be. Unlike other men's cum, his tasted salty *and* sweet, a yummy combination. Hungry for his flavor, she sucked him dry, then licked him until no trace remained.

His arm hung over his eyes, his face crimson, chest pumping.

She stroked his hairy leg. "You all right?"

He smacked his lips and nodded. "Never been better. Thanks. Now it's your turn."

Still gasping, he pushed up and hauled her onto him, his cock between her legs, pressed against her panties. "Get naked."

She wanted nothing more, but reality stopped her. "Can't."

His lust evaporated. He huffed. "Why not? Didn't I climax the way you like? Did you want me to moan louder or shriek? Should I have passed out? Would you have preferred — "

"Shh." She pressed her fingers against his lips. "We have to get ready and leave for the café."

He glanced at the closed blinds. "It's still dark."

"We have to prep the food before I can cook it."

His mouth turned down. "Can't you do that after we finish fucking? I swear, it won't take longer than twenty minutes. Thirty tops."

She'd definitely hit the jackpot. "You can last that long before coming?"

"If I'm inside your pussy I can."

Although tempting as fuck, she had to be strong. "Once the café closes for the night, I'm holding you to that." She poked his chest. "For now, though, we need to get ready and leave."

"Get ready how?"

"Shower for one. You know, wash ourselves."

"Can we do that together and wash each other?"

Out of the question, except it would make things go faster. "Follow me."

She rolled off him and dashed to the bathroom, him on her heels. Inside, she flipped on the light, took his hand, and froze. Numerous bruises covered his arms, torso, and legs, each mean looking and growing darker. "What happened last night?" His beer-scented breath blasted her each time he exhaled. "Did you fall down when you got drunk?"

"No matter how much I drink, I never get wasted." He regarded his bruised arm. "You did this."

"How? When?"

"Remember shaking my bottle before you opened it?" He wagged his finger. "I was inside, growling and trying to claw my way out before you did too much harm."

She cupped his face. "I didn't know. I'm so sorry. I didn't mean—"

"It's over. Let's do this."

He stripped her faster than she ever had, then ogled her naked breasts and the dark curls between her legs. "I like your bush." He cupped it. "I'm glad you don't shave there like some women do."

His previous liaisons weren't something she wanted to hear about now. She slumped against him, her bones dissolving each time he was near. "Have you ever showered before?"

"Countless times, since they've been invented. I've even taken a bubble bath." He scowled. "Didn't much like the bubbles." He gestured to the glass-enclosed tub. "Shall we?"

They soaped each other, using her apple-scented body wash.

His smile turned delirious. "Everything about you smells good."

She could sniff his thatch and male equipment for hours. She kissed him so hard, he lost his balance, his shoulder and ass hitting the tiled wall.

He pulled his mouth free, then switched positions with her. "Don't move."

"If I do?"

A roguish smile added danger to his rough good looks. "I may have to punish you."

"You'd better."

Laughing, he sank to his knees, separated her legs, and latched his mouth onto her clit.

Gawd. His tongue was hotter than her clay oven, damper than her pussy, and more satisfying than a swim on a sizzling afternoon. She shot to her toes, then dropped to her heels, her legs watery, breathing damn near impossible.

He held her nub between his teeth and licked slowly but ruthlessly, giving her no quarter. With one hand cupping her butt cheek, he slid his other down the furrow and teased her anus.

She juddered, her cunt eager for release.

He wouldn't give it, playing her expertly, bringing her close to the edge only to let her hang there unappeased.

She dug her fingers into his scalp. "Let. Me. Come."

He stopped licking her nub. "When I'm ready."

"Now."

"No." He rubbed his nose in her curls.

She drooped, her knees striking his shoulders.

On a lusty grunt, he resumed his carnal assault. Hell, he fucking owned her, using her clit as he desired, pushing her to the precipice and over the side.

She gasped and shivered at her climax, her limbs jelly, thoughts muddled.

Before she fell, he stood, pulled her into his arms, and caressed her gently. "You like?"

The question she'd asked him yesterday. Too drained to speak, she released her weight into him, inviting him to comfort her.

He didn't disappoint as he stroked her back and buried his face in her hair. "Sure you want to wait for the main event?"

Every cell in her hungered for him, but someone had to be practical in this. "I don't want to rush pleasure."

"Hmm." He eased back and lifted her chin. "You want me

to earn it first."

"I want us both to."

After they toweled off, his clothes became a problem, since he didn't have any. Luckily, Matt had left his stuff there. Who needed old duds when he could buy new ones using the thousands he'd stolen from her bank account?

Matt's jeans were too short on Jez, the tee too tight, and the shoes a struggle for him to pull on. At last, he simply stuffed his feet into them.

She squeezed his shoulder. "Once the afternoon rush ends, I'll run out and buy you stuff that fits. Can you make it that long? Do you want me to wish for your clothes?"

He turned his sneer from the ill-fitting mocs to her. "No."

Suit yourself. "Now for your hair."

He touched it. "What do you mean?"

"You need to pull it back and wear a hairnet around food. Health regulations."

He complained about having to look like a girl, but once they reached her café, he let her tie his locks back and didn't fight her on the net.

Confident he was on her side — at least as far as working here — she gave him the simplest task. "These are sweet potatoes." She held one in each hand. "You need to wash these, then cube them. When you're finished, there are fifty or so more you need to do the same thing to."

He stopped stroking her hip. "What's cube?"

She put the potatoes down and held up a knife. "Using this, you cut them into strips, then into squares — after you wash them."

He didn't take the vegetables or the blade. "Can't your patrons eat them as they are?"

"Not if I want to stay in business." Who knew how long that would last? "I'm making boniatillo, that's sweet potato pudding, for dessert. My lunch crowd loves it. Go on. Help me . . . in any way you can."

He gave her a look that said she was angling for a wish.

Guilty as charged. Why put them through this agony when he could easily have her wish for fully prepared food, and to have the café in the black financially?

Muttering, he grabbed the knife and speared the first potato.

"No, no, no." She took it from him. "You have to wash it first."

"I will. I'm using the knife to hold it under the water." He glanced around. "Where is it?"

The sink was to his side. Maybe she was expecting too much from him. Or he was playing dumb like many men did when they loathed doing a particular chore. She slid the potato off the blade and slapped it in his hand. "Wash it before you even think to use a knife. Go on." She gestured him toward the sink, then tackled the prep for her complicated dishes.

Her two other cooks shuffled in, both looking hung over but smiling through the pain.

She trusted them with her life and definitely her business. They were great cooks and never let her down. She winked at Raul who was razor thin despite the calories he devoured during his shifts. Stefano's weight would make a sumo wrestler envious. He didn't apologize for his size or enjoying his and her cooking. Nor should he. Whatever made him happy. She dipped her head in greeting.

Both men looked at Jez, curiosity on their faces, especially when they eyed his bruised arms.

She was afraid to introduce the men, considering Jez might tell them stuff no one should know. Until she had a word with him about keeping their secret, it was best not to let him talk to anyone.

Not that he seemed eager for chitchat. He was too busy swearing each time he dropped the potatoes, chased them across the floor, had to rewash them . . .

She turned on the radio. A Cuban timba played. The island music appropriated some R&B, salsa and other genres for a peppy tune. Stoked for the day, she diced, chopped, and worked her magic on the lunch fare.

By the time she'd finished the meat prep, there was just enough time to start the boniatillo. Even a novice like Jez would have cubed enough potatoes to make a sizeable batch.

She left her station and winced at the puny stack he'd completed. Enough to fill one dessert dish. She hurried to him. "What are you doing?"

"Working." Sweat dotted his face, his damp tee clung to his back, and food particles dirtied his bib apron. He held a sweet potato cube between his thumb and forefinger. "This one's perfect on all sides. I'll have to start over on the others to get them to look as good."

She put her hand on his chest to stop him from reaching for them. "They don't have to be even everywhere. I'm cooking them down. They won't have a form."

He slouched. "Now you tell me."

Jesus, this was a nightmare. "Just do your best. Work fast, please."

He cut and diced with too much abandon, slicing his fingers several times.

After sanitizing and bandaging his latest wound, she figured this was going to be one long day, the wishes more needed than ever.

CHAPTER THREE

Shortly after noon, Cari gave up on Jez prepping any food, no matter how simple, and had him wash dishes since the usual guy called in sick.

Racket from shattering plates and glasses drew the wait-staff into the kitchen. The two women gawked at him, blooms in their cheeks, sin in their eyes.

Cari joined them. "Ladies."

Twenty-something Veronica nodded in greeting, her gaze riveted to his ass. Middle-aged Ines was oblivious to every-thing except his broad back, then his face as he lost his grip on a wet plate and struggled to catch it.

Once he had, he leaned against the sink, breathing hard, muscles flexing.

Ines clapped. Veronica gave him a thumbs up.

Cari ushered them to the hallway that led to the dining room. Patrons' animated conversations and laughter flowed back here. "He's new and shy, so I'd appreciate if you wouldn't go into the kitchen any longer."

The ladies exchanged a glance. Veronica spoke first. "How will we get the orders to bring to the customers?"

Good question. "You can go in there, but don't stare at or talk to him, all right?"

"That's gonna be hard." Ines hugged her ample figure. "He's one hot dude."

Veronica wound a reddish tress around her finger. "Defi-nitely smokin'. What I could do with him . . ." Sighing, she closed her eyes. Her false eyelashes made long shadows on her youthful cheeks. "I'll definitely have to go to confession tomorrow."

She and Ines laughed.

Cari lumbered back to the kitchen. Once she'd finished the last order for the noon rush, she hurried to him. Thankfully, he hadn't broken anything during the last half hour. "How are you doing?"

He frowned at the dirty plates awaiting him. "The Inquisition wasn't this bad."

She went cold, then hot, hoping Stefano and Raul hadn't overheard.

They worked efficiently at their stations, their attention on the food, not him.

She leaned close and kept her voice low. "You were around during those times? Wait. What's wrong with your legs?" They bent outward.

"Nothing's wrong." He limped to the left and grabbed the first plate, then hobbled back to the sink.

"Do your feet hurt?"

"Nope. They went numb a few hours back."

God. She grabbed his hand. "Come with me."

"Where? I can't walk far or fast."

"I know." She slipped her arm around his waist. "I'll take it easy."

Snails progressed at a quicker pace, but she finally led him into her small office, locked the door, and helped him into her chair.

His head fell back. He sucked in several breaths.

On her knees, she pulled off his shoes and gasped. His feet were red and swollen, the toes purple. "Oh my God, why didn't you say something about this?"

"I was too busy trying to get stuff right." He lifted his head, then let it drop forward. "I didn't. I kept fucking up."

You poor baby. "Nonsense. You were fine." She rubbed his

battered feet. "That feel good?"

He opened one eye and looked at her. "You on my lap would be better."

No kidding. However, she had a business to run. "Later."

"Now. We earned this. No arguments or you'll regret it."

His tone had changed from agonized to frisky.

She shouldn't have played along, but she was only human, passion singing in her blood, her heart racing. "Yeah?" She gave him a cool look. "Dream on."

"Bad, bad girl." In one fluid and powerful move, he hauled her over his legs and paddled her ass.

She yelped, then pressed her mouth to his calf, muffling any future sounds. The biting stings transformed to soothing warmth. Sluggish, she let him do what he willed, loving it.

On a ragged breath, he finished and settled her on his lap, facing him. "No lip, understand?" He kissed her hard, deep, and long.

Dayum. Moisture seeped from her pussy, dampening her panties and jeans.

Deftly, he slipped his hands beneath her tee and undid her bra.

Before her boobs fell free, she pulled her mouth from his and gripped his lacerated wrists. "Hold on."

"Not for a second." He twisted from her grip, worked the button on her jeans, and lowered the fly. "We've waited too long already. We *earned* this."

"I'm not arguing. But I have to tell the staff not to bother us. Give me a sec, please."

He narrowed his eyes. "You have one minute."

"I'll work as fast as I can." She climbed off him and pressed the intercom button on her phone.

"Yeah?" Ines cleared her throat. "What's up?"

His cock, given the colossal bulge between his legs. "Can you send Veronica to my office?"

"Sure thing."

Cari grabbed her purse, pulled out the company credit card, and gave him a warning look. "Don't move or come to the door."

"I will if you don't return. You have thirty seconds."

She loved when he was alpha.

Footfalls sounded in the hall.

Before Veronica reached the office, Cari shot out the door. "I need you to go to the nearest clothing store for guys." She slapped the credit card in her hand. "Get several tees, a pair of jeans, and underwear, plus shoes, size fifteen."

Veronica's reddish eyebrows kept lifting. "Is this for the new guy?"

"I'm trying to help him out. He's had a tough time. When you come back, leave the bags outside this door."

"Okay. What size underwear should I get?"

She would focus on that. "Tell the clerk you want the clothes for a man who's six-four and one-ninety to two-hundred pounds. Lean but muscular . . . very muscular."

Her eyelashes fluttered. "I'll say. Should I hurry?"

"Uh-uh. Be back in an hour, that's all I ask. Also, please tell Ines and the others I won't be available during that time."

"You got it. Have fun. I sure as hell would."

"What?"

Giggling, she ran into the kitchen, presumably to tell the guys what Cari had said.

Back in her office, she locked the door.

Good thing. Jez was wonderfully nude, his dick cocked and ready for action, the swelling in his feet down considerably, though his toes were still maroon. "Standing doesn't bother you?"

"I have other things on my mind." He stalked to her.

She met him halfway, excited as fuck and trembling from need. "Me, too."

Together, they ditched her clothes and hairnet in record time even as they kissed. Quite a feat.

He hoisted her to his chest, her legs around his hips, her arms over his shoulders.

Rather than returning to the chair, he backed her into the wall and lifted his cock to her cunt. "Ready?"

She'd waited a lifetime for this and him. Somehow, Ethyl had known and had bequeathed her Jez, a guy who was one in a zillion. *Thank you.* Close to tears yet grinning like a loon, she had nothing to offer except the truth. "If I was any wetter, I'd leave a trail."

He laughed.

She kissed his prominent Adam's apple.

A wanting moan poured from him.

Eager to indulge in his scent, she pressed her face to his neck and shivered at how awesome he smelled: musky and pure male. "By the way, I'm on the pill, so no worries."

"I never had any. Jinns aren't born. They just are and don't reproduce."

Maybe. Maybe not. For him—and her—she wanted to leave every option open. "We're talking too much."

She claimed his mouth.

He still took charge, his tongue filling her, his cock plunging deep inside her cunt, their curls touching.

Mercy, mercy, mercy. His girth and length practically impaled her, the pressure intense but wondrous. Never had she known anything to match this.

His strength astounded, his thrusts aroused.

He took his time, leisurely sliding in and out of her while stroking her clit.

Delight spilled from her pussy to her inner thighs, then touched her pebbled nipples and settled in her throat. She gasped and gripped him as hard as she could.

In return, he increased his pace a fraction and kissed her

longingly.

She didn't play dead. With him, no sane woman could. She suckled his tongue, and each time he retreated, she tightened her inner muscles around his dick to increase the friction between them.

He tensed. His breathing hitched. He drove into her faster and harder, burying his cock, taking what was his.

What she'd given him.

Their fucking made a racket, her shoulders and ass hitting the wall. To her relief, the Latin music dampened the noise.

He growled and groaned, the sounds vibrating against her lips. Each time he pulled in air, his chest bumped hers and her nipples poked his pecs.

They went at each other like wild animals, no desire too crude or wanton, his grunts bordering on obscene, her whimpers depraved.

His cock thickened exponentially, and her glutted pussy narrowed further, adding to the magic, threatening to undo her.

No, no, no. She didn't want to come. Better to drag this out past the dinner hour, clear through tomorrow.

As she fought completion, she gripped his hair. The net tore. She grasped his ponytail. The ribbon she'd used to secure it came loose.

He pounded into her and rubbed her clit hard, lightly, then back to firm, keeping her off balance and breathless.

Two could play this game. She squeezed her sheath around his cock, then relaxed only to clasp him anew. Each action blended into the other until she lost track, her ears rang, and climax lashed her, the pleasure merciless and fucking welcomed.

She pulled her mouth from his and collapsed, her cheek hitting his jaw, breaths halting, a pulse beating crazily in her cunt. "Holy hell, you nearly killed me. *Thank you.*"

He kept pumping.

Given the way his cock stretched her cunt, he was still hard.

She gripped his shoulders. "You didn't come?"

"Not yet." He panted. "Not for a long while."

At least twenty minutes. Maybe thirty.

His complexion was brick red, his eyes wild, muscles twitching.

Despite his state, he carried her to the chair—his thrusts continual and zealous—dropped onto the seat, then jerked his hips to enter her as far as he could go.

Freaking spectacular. Even so . . ."Hey." She cradled his cheek. "Easy."

His eyes rolled back into his head, yet he kept pumping. "Am I hurting you?"

On each thrust, his shaft rubbed her nub, enticing her to another orgasm. "No. It feels great. I'm worried about you."

"Don't be. As long as you had fun." He gulped air. "You did, right?"

Her cunt still pulsed around his cock. "Don't you know?"

His proud smile gave him away. "I'd like you to tell me."

Her heart and soul opened to him. When he dropped the macho act and allowed himself to be vulnerable, he was so cute. "It—you—were beyond awesome, straight into legend-ary."

He beamed, then struggled for a breath. "Good to hear. Hang on."

Jez had promised Cari a prolonged ride and, by god, he intended to give her everything he had even if he passed out during the act.

Uh-uh. You can't. She thinks you're the man.

He couldn't disappoint her, especially now.

Her thighs hugged his, her kiss revealed intense passion

and ecstasy, and her heated depths caressed his cock as no other woman's had. For some reason, he and she fit. She got him . . . somewhat.

At least she hadn't complained about the fucked-up potatoes or broken dishes. Instead, she'd rubbed his feet.

How great was that?

Thankful, he sucked her tongue farther into his mouth, but still fought his natural urge to come.

Bad move. His balls felt as if she'd kicked them, his cock seemed twice its normal size.

He wasn't complaining. Another inch or two never hurt any man.

Pacing himself, he glided in and out of her pussy at a speed that wouldn't ratchet up his lust to an intolerable level.

Sweat poured down him. His calves and feet cramped.

The excruciating pain was a welcomed relief, deflating his dick somewhat and giving him a breather.

She licked his nipple, then sucked his pec, leaving heated bursts in her wake.

His cock revved back to full alert in two seconds flat.

To battle against climax, he ran crappy memories in his mind. Those nasty Inquisition days were the worst, especially when the robed priests tried to burn him at the stake. Thankfully, they couldn't, because he turned to smoke. To this day, no other humans had freaked out as they had.

And what about Mr. Kremp's wrinkled body? He didn't have a navel either, at least one Jez could see. Too much loose skin covered it.

Then there was . . .

Cari pumped up and down his cock, taking up the slack he didn't realize he'd provided.

Her ebony hair bounced, and her numerous earrings slapped her jawline and cheeks.

Damn, her jewelry was adorable.

Her areolas puckered, making the tips seem longer. There wasn't one scar, freckle, or misplaced mole on her creamy flesh, her skin so youthful and dewy, it made him batty.

He grabbed her hips to slow her down.

No good. She bounced against him like a piston, her eyes closed, mouth hung open.

On a lusty shriek, she threw back her head and came.

So did he.

Shit. Crap. Fuck. It was too soon but stopping now was like trying to hold back a sneeze.

Extraordinary feelings thundered through him, turning him inside out, flinging him up, down, sideways, then squeezing out his last breath.

He gasped.

She fell against him, her huffs warming his chest, her vibrating cunt sucking his cock deeper inside.

Although he wanted to thank her, speech eluded him, as did movement, his arms too heavy to lift.

Sprawled on the chair with her snuggled close, he gave into blessed slumber.

Sharp knocks sounded.

Cari flinched, unable to identify where the noise had originated. The warm skin beneath her was also a mystery.

Wait – Jez.

They'd fallen asleep. For how long?

More knocks on her door.

She cleared her throat and tried to sound awake. "Yes?"

"I got your stuff." Veronica giggled, sounding excited. "Hope he doesn't mind wearing stretchy boxed briefs. You know, the sexy kind."

"Huh?" He stirred and cuffed Cari's wrist. "Hey, where are you going?" He hauled her back onto his lap and pressed his face in her hair. "I didn't give you the full half hour. Not that

I didn't try, but you were a bad girl, pushing me past the point of no return. You know what that means."

He swatted her ass.

The crack sounded deafening.

"Ah, Cari?" Veronica tried the knob. It rattled but didn't open. "You okay?"

She pressed her hand over his mouth. "Busy. I'm going over next week's schedule and payroll."

"Oh hey, don't let me stop you. I put the card and receipt inside a sock. They're in the smallest bag."

"Great. Thanks."

The moment Veronica's footfalls faded, Cari pushed off him and jogged away from his reach. "We have to get back to work." She kept her voice low. "You need to put on your new clothes."

He stroked his cock and fondled his balls. "I prefer skin."

What else? She blew hair off her face. "Do you want me to be in the mood tonight after we leave here?"

"Okay, okay, I get it." He jumped from the chair, winced, then stood on the sides of his feet.

Aw, baby, I'm sorry about your poor toes, the wrist lacerations, and your sliced fingers. If he stayed here much longer, he'd be in traction. After dressing hurriedly, she lugged in the bags.

The clothes fit like they'd been made for him. She helped with the shoes. "Easy now. No need to rush."

"There is, if I intend to earn what goes on tonight between you and me."

She lowered the shoe, shame gripping her. "Hey, I didn't mean for that to apply to sex. What we did a few minutes ago happened because I wanted it and you."

Gratitude and affection softened his features. "Yeah? Same here. Is it okay if we take a second to hug?"

There wasn't a thing on Earth she wanted more. Pushed to her knees, she eased him into her arms.

He caressed her tenderly, as if she were precious and

mattered.

Her throat tightened. She embraced him in return, not trying to hide the love she felt. It was far too soon for such intense emotions, but she couldn't stop them. Didn't want to.

They kissed, a gentle and heartfelt journey as they bonded, female to male, lover to loved.

She cupped his ass.

He lowered her fly.

They were hopeless. She yanked free. "We're doing it again."

He smiled and rested his forehead against hers. "I don't mind."

"I know." She smacked his ass. "But you have dirty dishes to see to."

He groaned. "Isn't there something else I can work on?"

"Do you know how to do books? If so, have at it. I hate accounting."

"I might, too, if I knew what it is."

Dishes it was. "Tell you what, I'll teach you. But for now . . ." She pulled him from her office into the kitchen.

If Jez never saw another dirty plate for the rest of eternity, he'd be a happy guy.

Water drenched the sink, counter, his apron, tee, and jeans. The feeling had returned to his feet, leading to pain worse than what he'd endured on the rack during the Dark Ages. He should have turned to smoke then, but wanted to see what the screams and shrieks were about.

Definitely not a day at Disney World.

Exhausted but finished for the day, he dragged to Cari's office.

She gripped her chair, worry pinching her features, her gaze on numerous papers.

Although everyone else had left for the evening, he closed the door behind himself. "You all right?"

She started, looked at him, then away. "Yeah. Fine."

A lie. She chewed her lip and drew in her shoulders.

Whenever a mortal behaved as she did, the individual expected a blow or something worse.

He crouched by her chair.

She offered a wan smile. "Want to sit? Are your feet any better?" She glanced at them.

"I'd like you to tell me what's wrong."

"Nothing." She pushed the papers away.

He brought them back. Although he could read, he didn't understand what the symbols represented or why the numerous figures would upset her. "What are these?"

"Today's receipts. The money we made."

"Wow." He grinned. "Look at how many there are. Like hundreds."

"Three twenty, to be precise."

"That's amazing."

"Uh-huh." Her eyes filled.

"Don't cry, please." He wound his arm around her shoulders. "Tell me why three twenty isn't good. Were you hoping for less? More?"

She sniffed and ran her finger beneath her nose. "The take's good, but it's not enough to cover the rent on this place and my apartment. I'm still short several hundred dollars."

Buying him clothes and shoes hadn't helped. "We can take my stuff back." He touched his tee. "I don't need it. I can wear Mutt's stuff."

She snickered. "Matt. No, you can't. Your clothes won't make a dent in my debt."

"What if we work harder?"

She folded her arms on the desk and lowered her head to them. "I'm already here sixteen hours, seven days a week. I can't give anymore." Her shoulders trembled. "I'm going to lose this place, I know it."

"Please don't say that." He rubbed her back. "What if you talk to the people you owe? Ask them for more time?"

"I already have."

"I haven't."

She shot to a sitting position and grasped his tee. "No way. I do not want you exposing yourself to the public. *Do you hear me?*"

The people in the next building probably had. He pried her death grip off his top. "I wouldn't tell them I'm a jinn. I'd intimidate them in another way."

She dropped back and covered her eyes.

He scoured his brain for a better solution and had it. "You could sell my bottle. I'm sure it's worth something."

She shook her head. "That's your home."

"Trust me, it's not that great. Tiny, dark, stuffy . . ."

Laughter poured from her and turned to a whimper. "It's still the only place you've known."

Concern gnawed at him. "Are you saying that because you want me to stay there rather than with you?"

"No!" She kissed his knuckles and palm, carefully avoiding his many cuts. "I want you with me."

He breathed easier, struggled for another suggestion, then grinned. "Have you tried a GoFundMe account?" Mr. Kremp's youngest maid used one to raise funds for her implants when he wouldn't give her a raise.

Cari released his hand. "How do you know about crowdfunding?"

"It worked for Francine."

She pushed back. "Who?"

"Mr. Kremp's maid. She wanted bigger tits. Double Ds, at least." He cupped his pecs as if he was holding them up. "My master was too cheap to buy them for her and wouldn't wish for them either, letting me help. He suggested she beg for the money online. He did warn her to avoid saying she wanted a boob job. Apparently, that's not cool. He told her to say she was dying and —"

"Oh my god, stop." She rubbed her temple. "Your masters sound like pricks."

"I don't miss them." He squeezed her knee. "I would you. A lot."

Her chin quivered.

Not new tears. "I'm not going anywhere, and bad shit is not going to happen." He used his harshest tone. "We'll work this out. You're tired and you need rest. Once you sleep, you'll think more clearly. Come on." He pulled her from the chair, carried her out of the office and building, then to her apartment.

The trek didn't do his back and feet any good, but having her sleep rather than cry or worry was worth his discomfort.

At her place, he tucked her into bed, yearning to join her. Hell, he needed to make love to her, but didn't try. She'd worked harder today than anyone at the restaurant, especially him. Until these last hours, he'd had no idea how difficult her life was. Upon meeting her, he'd assumed she had it made. She was free to do as she pleased, could come and go as she wished, always had food and drink available, and a future that opened in every direction rather than leading to an endless, servile existence like his.

He didn't feel sorry for himself any longer. His concern centered on her. She'd had a rough day and deserved some peace.

He retreated to the kitchen. Unable to find another six-pack, he settled for red wine.

With the bottle in hand, he lay on the sofa, drinking and brainstorming, trying to devise a plan to bring her the extra bucks she needed.

He fell asleep at 2 AM, no answer in sight.

Cari padded into the living room at 4:30. "What are you doing out here?"

Aching and yawning. "I didn't want to disturb you. Did you sleep well?"

She stopped, scratching her hip. "Like I died. But we didn't play."

God love her, she wanted him. He hoped as a person, not merely a stud. *Who am I kidding?* At this point, he craved her so badly, he'd accept anything she'd give. "We will tonight, promise. Also during the day, at lunch."

She wagged her finger. "The staff will talk."

"Do you care?"

Laughter shook her shoulders and boobs. "No. We better get going."

Her good mood held through their morning shower and the walk to the café, then took a nosedive when she opened her office door.

He should have hidden the receipts so they wouldn't upset her. "How about we have our mine and croquetas now? They're still warm."

She plopped in her chair. "You go ahead. I'm not hungry. In fact, do you mind getting started on your day?"

His spirits sank. "Washing dishes?"

"You can slice and dice, too."

"My fingers?" Joking, he held up his maimed hands.

She tried to smile, but it didn't quite catch. "Just be careful, okay? And please don't tell Raul or Stefano that you're a jinn. That would fuck things up to a point I don't want to visit."

He'd cut off his balls before worrying her further. "I won't tell them anything, not even my name. Who are they?"

"The guys in the kitchen with you."

He nodded. "I'll keep my distance unless I need their

help."

"Thanks. Close the door?"

Doing so went against what he wanted, but the sorrow and concern on her face kept him from disagreeing.

Each time he had a moment to catch his breath, Jez hurried to the office, hoping to see Cari.

The door remained closed.

Several times, she spoke to someone, her voice too low to understand words, her mood dejected or edgy.

Unable to stand the turmoil, he approached the thin guy in the kitchen. "Hey, I'm Jez."

"Raul. Nice to meet you. I'd shake your hand, but . . ." He inclined his head to the uncooked food he held.

"That's okay. How much do you make?"

Raul's face blanched, which couldn't have been easy considering his dusky complexion and the intense heat in here. "Why? How much do you make?"

"Nothing. That's what I wanted to talk to you about. Would you be willing to forgo pay for say a couple of months?" That should easily get the extra funds.

He stared. "Are you serious? Hey man, I got a girlfriend and two kids to support. My babies aren't even in school yet. I need my paycheck." He stepped back and ran into the counter. "Is this place closing? Is that what you're trying to tell—"

"No. Forget what I said." This was harder than he considered. Humans went ballistic about the least little thing. "I'm trying to find a way to cut costs." A phrase Mr. Kremp always used.

Raul's mouth sagged open. "Is Cari going to fire me?"

"Not that I know of. You should ask her—Wait. Don't bother her. She's busy."

"Searching for my replacement?"

"No. Talking to her . . . uh . . . sister." Francine had one who'd also worked for Mr. Kremp.

Raul frowned. "I thought Cari was an only child."

"Could be she was talking to her brother. Sorry I bothered you." Jez would have questioned Stefano when he arrived, but worried how he might take working for nothing.

Maybe there was something in this place Cari could sell. The huge oven might bring in a few bucks. The plates and glasses he hadn't broken were nice. So was the dining area furniture.

Mrs. Kremp always bragged about selling the master's stuff on eBay without him knowing, until the items were long gone. She hid the proceeds in her underwear, a place she said he'd never look.

She was right. He didn't go anywhere near her lingerie or her.

Instead, he filed claims with his insurance company, saying burglars had stolen his things. The company always paid, making him richer.

Cari could do the same.

Eager to tell her, he rapped on her door.

Nothing.

He turned the knob. Locked. Not a good sign. "Hey, it's me." He rapped harder. "Let me in, please. I have something to tell you."

The door flew open. She tugged him inside, then closed and locked the door. "What happened? What did you do?"

He didn't much like the accusation in her voice. "Nothing. I was just thinking." He pushed out a breath. "I came up with a plan to save this place and your apartment."

Doubt filled her eyes.

He warned himself not to take her disbelief personally. If he'd faced the shit she had, he'd be in worse shape. "Do you want to hear it?"

"Ah, sure." She propped her hip against the desk. "Shoot."

The moment he mentioned eBay, she sank into her chair, elbows on her knees, head in her hands. When he brought up Mr. Kremp's claims, she groaned.

Patience. "You're not giving my idea a chance."

"If I did, I'd be accused of insurance fraud. That's what Mr. Kremp was involved in. People go to jail for that and serve long sentences. Jinns I'm not so sure about."

A wrinkle he hadn't considered. "You could ask your employees to work without pay."

She ground her fists into her eyes. "And have the state put me out of business? There are laws against slavery."

Right. He'd lived through that era. A nasty time. "Don't worry, I'll come up with something else, I swear."

"Thanks. I appreciate it." She patted his arm, then sighed. "However, nothing's going to work. I've called every vendor, plus the management companies that operate this building and my apartment. They won't budge. I have to get them what I owe by the end of next week. If I don't, it's over. Which it will be as I can't see how —"

"You could wish for it."

She stilled. "What?"

Age-old principles and tradition didn't mean anything if they hurt her. "I said you could make a wish for the money."

Her face brightened. She wept. "You'd do that for me? You'd *serve* me?"

In any fashion she wanted. He brushed away her tears. "Don't cry. Your unhappiness kills me."

"Sorry." She flapped her hand near her face. Like magic, her tears stopped. Her apprehension didn't. "You're sure you want to do this? If you break the jinn code and serve a woman, nothing bad will happen to you, will it?"

"No. Not me. However, there is a catch."

She clenched her chair. "Something awful will happen to me?"

"No!" Antsy, he paced, not knowing how to tell her the truth. He hadn't considered it would come up since he'd had no plans to serve her. "You and I will be fine. However . . ." He faced her. "No wish happens without consequences. Sometimes minor. Sometimes terrible . . . or deadly."

CHAPTER FOUR

Cari couldn't believe it.

Disgustingly rich bankers had tanked the economy to get more money they didn't need and not one had gone to jail. Politicians lied, cheated, and stole their way to power, hurting innocents in whatever manner they could, and they never lost their seats. Televangelists sinned more than every congregation member combined, yet they had private jets, mega-mansions, and designer clothes while the homeless population kept rising.

All she wanted was one lousy, freaking wish to honor her grandparent's memory by keeping this place in business and to pay her staff, who needed to make a living. Yet her heart's desire might prove deadly.

She squeezed her seat so hard she ripped the fake leather. "What? How—*why?*"

"I don't know." He gestured helplessly. "It's always been that way. There's no such thing as a free wish."

"Again, why? I'm not asking for the moon, just a little extra cash. Are you sure about this?"

He looked ill. "Every time my master, Mr. Kremp, wished for a young, beautiful maid to show up and agree to work for the lousy wages he paid—and believe me, they weren't even minimum, except by nineteen-forty standards—his wife, Mrs. Kremp, got hurt. When his wishes asked for the maids to screw around with him, it broke her heart."

"That lousy fucking bastard." She slammed her fist against her desk. "How dare he. Ethyl was so sweet."

58

"I know. I used to console her when she got down. She was like the grandmother I never had."

She left her chair and threw her arms around him. "I'm glad you were there to help out."

"I didn't much. She cried a lot. I hate to admit it, but I refused to grant her wishes for the same reasons I gave you. Also because she wanted me to raise Mr. Kremp from the dead, which I couldn't, so she could give him a piece of her mind. Let's just say, she wasn't happy when I kept saying no and she warned that someday I'd have to serve a female. Maybe sooner than I expected. No way did I believe her. Then you came along and . . ." He inhaled deeply and blew out his breath. "I didn't even know her first name until you said it. I'm a snake."

"You were confused about men's power. You're not any longer. You tried to comfort her. That's what matters." She hugged him. "I still don't understand, though."

He rubbed her back. "What don't you get?"

"How my wish for extra cash could turn out terrible. For who?"

"The bank your wish would take it from."

She recoiled. "You mean like stealing?"

"Unfortunately. Even if the money didn't come from a bank, it might from a person on the street who needed it as much as you do but didn't have it any longer because you got it."

That didn't make sense. "Can't my wish conjure new bills?"

"Wouldn't that be counterfeiting? The TV programs I watched with Mrs. Kremp warned against that."

Cari sagged, then straightened. "I could wish for my own stuff that Matt took, right?"

"Not exactly."

She gripped his biceps. "What's that mean?"

"You might get the money he already spent, which means taking it from an innocent merchant. Or he might have it in a bank, which means — "

"Right." She released him and rested her forehead against the wall. "Is there no way to get around this crap?"

"Not that I know of. Whatever you wish for has to come from something that already exists, meaning you have to take it from another individual or business or whatever. For example, if you wanted more customers here, they'd come from another restaurant which might cause it to close, screwing the owners and employees. If you chose to add extra years to your life, someone else would have to die earlier than they should have so you'd — "

"Stop." She couldn't listen any longer. "I could never do anything like that or the other stuff you said."

"I know, and I'm sorry the wishes aren't what you thought they were." He gathered her in his arms, her cheek on his shoulder. "Please don't give up. There has to be a way to fix this. I'll do my level best to help you any way I can, even if you do want a wish."

His kindness and worry touched her in places she hadn't allowed herself to acknowledge for years. First, when her mother chose partying and drugs over her, then when her grandparents died, and finally when Matt had used her so ruthlessly.

She hugged Jez. "It's okay. No matter what happens, I won't give you to anyone else . . . unless you want to leave me."

"Never." He held her as hard as she did him.

They clung to each other as if the world were ending.

Her small part in it might be, but at least she had him. No guy could match his good heart, fair play, sexy moves, killer face and bod . . .

Wait.

Every woman who saw him, whether in the café or on the

street, always stopped, rubbernecked, then drooled. Effortlessly, he drew females to him.

An idea formed. She cupped his head. "How do you feel about having women stare at you?"

He blinked. "What do you mean?"

"Would that bother you?"

"Are you asking if I would feel like a piece of meat?"

That's what she'd been going for. Her growing enthusiasm waned. "Forget what I said. I would never want you to feel—"

"You're the only one who could hurt me when it comes to my looks. Especially if they're the only reason you desired me, or because of the wishes I could grant, rather than liking me for the person I am."

"No way!" She embraced him. "The other stuff doesn't matter. It's you I want. You're sweet, kind, generous—"

"Then I don't give a fuck what other women think. Let them look." He eased back, confusion on his face. "Why would they look?"

"I have an idea on how to bring in the funds we need."

Once she had color flyers printed showing lunch and dinner specials, she stationed Jez outside the café. His new job was to hand out the advertisements. And to be himself: tall, dark, gorgeous, and easygoing.

Women, young, old, and in-between, flocked to his side. He listened to whatever they said and teased when the conversation warranted it, which lured them in further. When he asked them to consider the specials, they did.

Ninety-nine percent came inside and ordered what he'd suggested.

The other one-percent returned after they'd gone to ATMs to get the needed cash.

She considered having a machine installed in the

restaurant.

Within days, the place had more customers than it ever had. By the weekend, she had enough funds to pay the rent there and at her apartment, with hundreds left over.

She gave everyone, including Jez, a bonus.

He took to his new job with a fervor seen only in the faithful hell-bent on proselytizing.

New patrons became regulars. Regulars bitched about having to wait in line for a seat.

She added tables and chairs outside, hired another cook, two more waitstaff, and extended the hours, even opening for breakfast. The food and Yelp reviews were so good, Jez didn't have to use his natural charm to drag additional customers in. Not even women.

As much as Cari hated to admit it, she didn't much like countless females fawning over him, even if he remained polite yet distant, flirtatious but ever faithful to her.

Nightly, they played carnal games in her apartment, including kink.

She loved submission and spanking, her pretend defiance making his cock harder than titanium.

This evening, he gestured to the kitchen table. "Bend over that face down, ass high, legs spread."

Her pussy went nuts, moisture bathing it, her sheath throbbing from need. "No."

He strode to her, muscles rippling, power oozing from every pore. "What did you say?"

She squared her shoulders.

His gaze fell to her naked breasts.

Her nipples tightened. "I'll never obey you. You'll have to tie me up first."

He wrapped his hand around her neck and held her lightly but used enough strength to keep her from fleeing. "Wish for it. Now. Or else."

"Or else what?"

"You won't get this." He kissed her as if he meant it and drove three fingers into her cunt.

Her legs got rubbery.

When he'd had his fill, he lifted his face.

If not for his fingers still inside her, she would have dropped to the floor. "Yes, Master. I wish to be tied up, using stuff in my apartment."

Instantly, bras wrapped around her wrists and ankles. An invisible force secured her to the table, and a dishtowel covered her eyes.

Blindfolded and helpless, she could only wait. Her pulse sprinted, heat poured through her, and her skin grew damp.

He padded around the table.

She supposed it was to take her in from every angle.

His breaths quickened, matching hers. He halted and swatted her butt. "Assume the position I demand."

Fuck, this rocks. Slavish to his order, she lifted her ass.

He touched her cunt, then her anus, indicating he'd use both tonight. He wouldn't spare any opening she owned when it came to his pleasure.

Without warning, he mounted her vaginally, his thrusts unrestrained, thumb on her clit.

Ah . . .

He brought her to a quick climax and left her gasping.

As she struggled to breathe, he sheathed himself, lubed her anus, and mounted her, the pressure acute but divine.

She bucked, driving into him, wanting every-damn-thing he could give.

He rode her long, his thrusts unyielding, but didn't come until she climaxed twice more.

Once they'd finished, he pulled out and spanked her, as she liked, then pressed his mouth to her ear. "Wish us into bed."

She did, where they made love missionary style, gazes

locked, smiles wide, as they burrowed deeper into each other's heart and soul.

Nothing could stop them now. The restaurant was in the black several times over. Her bank account had never been healthier. Jez couldn't stop grinning.

Neither could she, realizing Ethyl's endowment was in response to a wish Cari had held in her heart for years. To have a man who cherished and respected her. Who couldn't live without her at his side.

Hand-in-hand, she and Jez returned to the restaurant from their run to a new produce vendor. He'd haggled with the poor woman until she caved to the price he wanted.

What a guy. "I hope you know what your reward is for saving us twenty percent."

He opened the front door. "You'll tie me up in the kitchen or to the bed, possibly both?"

She laughed. He didn't. She sobered. "You're serious?"

"Yep." He chucked her chin. "Why should you have all the fun?" He pressed his mouth to her ear. "I thought we might try cuffs and a leather belt, too—nothing extreme, just enough to pump up the action."

She squeezed his fingers. "You're on."

Veronica ran up. "Guys, there's a man here to see Jez."

That didn't sound right. A woman, Cari understood, but a man . . ."Did he say who he is or what he wants?"

"No. He's over there." She pointed.

The man left his seat and approached, his skin sallow, suit black and gloomy, features funereal. He couldn't be an undertaker for jinns. They never died.

Upon seeing the man, Jez's face went white.

Alarmed, she pressed against him. "Do you know who he is?"

"Mr. Kremp's nephew."

"Kremp, your last master?"

Veronica gave Cari a weird look.

Shit. She had to watch her big mouth. "Table fourteen is waving you over. Do you mind seeing what they need?"

"On it." She trotted away.

The nephew reached them. Ignoring her, he spoke to Jez. "You're coming with me."

What? "Like hell he is." She stood between the turd and Jez. "What's this about?"

Several customers stopped eating and looked at them.

She spoke to the jerk. "If you want to talk, fine." She kept her voice low. "But we'll do so in my office. Otherwise, I'm calling the cops."

"You don't want to do that." He frowned at Jez. "Does she?"

Jez pulled her behind himself. "If you dare hurt her—"

"Come with me and I won't have to."

"Fuck this." She spoke to the creep. "Don't force my hand out here. There are too many knives around."

His ghastly complexion got chalkier. He smoothed his jacket. "Very well. We can speak, but it won't change anything."

It had to, even though she didn't know what this concerned.

Once in the office, she locked the door, turned the radio up so no one could overhear, then got in Mr. Jerk's face.

He stepped back and hit her chair.

It rolled away.

She cornered him. "How dare you come to my business and threaten me."

He arched one bushy eyebrow. "I only want what's mine." He pointed at Jez.

Anguish filled his eyes, his reaction scaring her. She touched his arm. "What's this about?"

Kremp spoke first. "Upon my aunt's death—"

"Ethyl?"

"Yes. When she passed, the jinn was supposed to go to me."

"You mean Jez." Cari poked the SOB's chest. "He has a name. Use it."

His ugly face grew mean. "He has wishes that belong to me, no one else. He's been in the Kremp family for generations. He's rightfully mine. My aunt had no business giving him to you."

"Maybe not. But you can't have him." She squeezed Jez's fingers, hoping to convince him everything would be all right. "Possession is nine-tenths of the law."

"Only until I win my lawsuit against you." He tugged on his lapels. "I'll drag you through every court in this country. Trust me, I have the funds to do so and more. I'll ruin you financially. You'll never dig yourself out of debt."

"Prick!" Jez rushed Kremp.

She yanked him back before he tore the douche apart. "You have enough money to fight me endlessly, more than you'll ever need, but you still want Jez? What's wrong with you?"

He looked as if she'd impugned his manhood. "No one can be too rich. It's not possible. Turn him over to me."

He held out his palm, as if they were exchanging an inanimate object, not a sentient being who cried, laughed, and dreamed the same as everyone else. Except for him.

Motherfucker. She punched his hand.

He gasped.

She squeezed her fists. "You're not going to do anything. What did you intend to tell the judges and juries? That you want your jinn back?"

"We'll battle over the priceless antique bottle he calls home. If anyone reveals that he's in there, and what he is, it will be you. Then you'll be able to watch the government treat him like a lab rat, experimenting to see what make a jinn tick."

"You goddamn bastard." She rushed him, eager to claw his face.

Before she could, Jez pulled her back and held her close. "Don't do anything to her. I'll come with you."

"No!" She held onto him. "You're not leaving me. I won't let you."

"Cari, please. It's all right. I don't want you hurt."

"By that *thing*?" She gestured to Kremp.

He grimaced, showing his yellow teeth. "It appears you two need a moment alone to work this out." His scowl deepened. "Make it fast. You have two minutes, tops. Then I'm calling my attorney and filing suit. And don't try anything funny. If you do, I'll include every employee here in my litigation, ruining them, too."

He slammed the door on his way out.

Cari grabbed Jez's arm. "Don't leave. I don't want to live without you."

Tears sparkled in his eyes. "I can't let you lose this place. It's your life."

"You are." She hugged him. "Nothing else matters. I have enough in savings to hire a good attorney."

"His will be better. Mr. Kremp, my master, sued people to get a hard on. He couldn't manage one another way. Not even his wishes helped for long. He never let up on his suits until he'd taken his victim's last penny. Even then, he wished for more stuff from me. His kind is never satisfied. It's a sickness."

Her stomach rolled, but her resolve hardened. "We'll run away." It was the only solution. "I can wish for us to disappear. Not literally. Figuratively. We'll go someplace he'll never find us."

"What about your café?"

She died a little at the thought of leaving it, but he was

more important.

He squeezed her shoulders. "What about the people here who count on you for a job?"

She'd forgotten about them. For once, she wanted to be selfish, not caring. "They'll find other employment."

"What if they don't? What if Kremp ruins them like he said? Raul has two kids, Stefano five. Ines is putting her daughter through college. Veronica's saving up to buy better wheels."

"He could be bluffing. Bullies are like that." She gripped his tee. "I can't sacrifice you for anything. I won't. If I make the wish, will you grant it? Do you have a choice?"

"You know I don't."

True. If she hadn't expected his answer, she wouldn't have asked the question. "Ready? Wait. Where should we go? Have you ever been to your native country? Where is it? Do you want to go there? Or would you prefer Paris or Spain? Do you speak their languages? If you do, will you teach—"

"Easy." He pressed his finger against her lips. "There might be another solution."

She pulled his hand away. "What?"

He glanced at the door then settled his mouth on her ear. "You can wish Mr. Kremp, the nephew, away."

As nice as that sounded, Jez's suggestion didn't comfort her. She pressed her mouth to his ear. "You mean make him vanish? Isn't that murder?"

A crazy question, but she had to know how far she'd go to save Jez. At this point, offing Kremp didn't seem so awful.

"No," he spoke quietly. "Wish for his memories about me to disappear, so he won't know who I am, and will split."

It could work. Damn, it had to. "Help me put together the words. We have one shot. I can't get this wrong."

They deliberated.

Footfalls sounded outside the door. Kremp pacing. Their

time running short.

Jez gripped her arms. "Do you have it?"

"Yeah." Her insides burned. "Ready?"

He nodded.

She let loose, saying what they'd agreed on, wishing as she never had before.

The pacing stopped.

Jez glanced at the door. "Stay here while I check what happened."

"Screw that." She hung onto his arm. "I'm coming with you."

Together they opened the door.

Kremp spun around and looked at them, his face blank. "Uh . . ."

Cari's heart pounded against her throat, making speech difficult. "Can I help you?"

He glanced into her office, then backed up. "Ah, no. I, uh, was trying to find the men's restroom."

Jez pointed. "That way. Do you want me to show you?"

She dug her nails into his arm, unwilling to release him.

He winced.

Kremp edged away. "No, I'm fine. Back there, you say?" He pointed behind himself. "Thanks." He disappeared from view.

She let out a whoop.

Jez laughed and hugged her.

EPILOGUE

Six months later . . .

Cari added the final changes to the new menu and handed it to Jez. "Look good?"

He scanned what she'd written. His stomach growled. "Is that enough of an answer?"

"Hardly." She patted his taut stomach. "You're always hungry."

"Only for you." He pulled her against him, adoration enriching his kiss.

Hers was no different. Time had drawn them closer. She told him about her mom doing meth. She hadn't been the greatest mother before then, but the drugs made her batshit crazy. The state had put Cari into foster care, forcing her grandparents to fight for her. Everyone said they were too old and didn't have enough time to raise a kid. They ignored the arguments, put the café in debt to hire attorneys, and adopted her.

Jez's past had been as bleak. One day he simply woke up, fully grown, but reduced to smoke and stuck in his bottle.

His first master treated him cruelly, beating him when the wishes weren't executed to his satisfaction. If Jez dared turn to smoke to avoid the blows, the master locked him in his bottle for months to break his spirit.

The others kept him hopping day and night, demanding the world, bellyaching when they didn't get it.

Those who wanted him to destroy another person were the

worst. He had to outwit them to avoid committing murder, then take the heat at their outrage.

He'd lived through appalling times and more hopeful ones like the Enlightenment and the sixties when ordinary people demanded their right to live and love like the elites.

Now he was here with her, their future something she no longer feared.

Weekly, they laid flowers on Ethyl's grave, thanking her for bringing them together.

Flush with cash, Cari rented a small house so they could frolic at will and get as shameless as they liked.

Their lust knew no end nor did their devotion.

He ended their kiss and held up the menu. "Time for me to drill the troops on this."

"You'd better."

She'd made him manager. The staff would have followed him to Hell and back. He had no equal in wrangling deals from vendors, freeing her to do what she loved most—cooking.

For now though, she had one last thing to do before ducking into the kitchen.

He glanced at the frame she held. "You're sure about this?"

"I'm proud of you." His picture couldn't have been hotter. "I want to brag."

"And direct complaints to me once they see my mug, name, and title displayed in the dining area."

"There aren't any complaints. We have a consistent five-star Yelp rating."

"Nothing's forever."

"This is." She took his hand. "And so are we."

Joyous beyond anything she'd expected, she led him from her office into their shared destiny.

The End

YOU MAY ALSO ENJOY THE FOLLOWING FROM EXTASY BOOKS INC:

Sensual Stranger
Tina Donahue

Excerpt

Toni Starr propped her shoulder against a storefront on the deserted street, ignoring her thirst, the heat, and her weariness. For too many years, she'd yearned for a place to call her own where she'd always belong.

Wouldn't happen in this small town.

Hopefully, the automotive service shop across the street would open before a merchant, or worse, a cop showed up and ran her off.

Please, not that. She couldn't walk another step.

The metal doors for Brody's Auto Repair rattled upward for the day's business.

Her pulse picked up.

A man inside the building gripped a clipboard holding numerous papers. The bays were empty except for cars, no other employees having arrived. Nor were there any customers waiting at the glass door in front.

An old Tim McGraw tune poured from inside, the singer's resonant voice subdued by heartache.

Her fatigue and uncertainty retreated, replaced by interest in the man. Surely over six feet, he looked early thirties or so and filled out his white cotton tee and worn jeans nicely.

She managed a small breath.

Solid didn't begin to address his broad shoulders, sculpted chest, and muscular biceps. Faded denim hugged his powerful legs, and the meaty bulge behind his fly.

Her mouth watered despite the worsening heat and the mess she was in.

He turned to the side, taking his best parts from her view.

Disappointed, she craned her neck.

Blond locks streaked his light brown hair, worn longish on the top and sides, wonderfully tousled as if he'd finger-combed it after he'd rolled out of bed.

He certainly hadn't shaved.

Short, dark bristles shadowed his cheeks, firm jaw, and upper lip, his beginning beard virile and wholly masculine, complementing his rich, sensuous mouth.

Her stomach fluttered, and her thoughts roamed at being in his strong arms, safe from hurt the world seemed determined to inflict. His big body pressed close, hard, and protective.

He strode to a Saturn in the middle bay, favoring his right leg. Not a limp exactly, more a hesitation in his fluid gait. The way a man would walk after straining the muscles in his calf.

Pain flickered across his handsome features, followed by what might have been sorrow or regret.

As quickly as the emotion surfaced, it passed. His face grew impassive, all business, his attention torn between the car and his clipboard, then something to the left in the work area. Crossing it, he again depended more on his right leg, stopped at a small refrigerator, and pulled out a bottled water. He placed it on a waist-high metal cabinet that likely held tools. Forearms on it, he bent his head to the papers, reading the first then the next.

She couldn't tell if he owned the place or simply managed

it. More importantly, whether he'd listen to her and have the authority to do what she needed.

Desperation returned. Perspiration trickled down her cheek. She squinted at the unforgiving sun streaming over distant mountains and past the flat-faced buildings on her side. Those rays hit the garage full-on, bathing it in the light, seeming to direct her.

Go on. Before anyone else shows up.

Queasy with uncertainty, she pushed away from the gift shop. The small downtown area was quiet, the other storefront businesses closed. No cars rolled down the narrow two-lane street. No locals or visitors noticed her. Nor did he. His focus remained on the papers, shoulders relaxed.

He pushed a wayward lock behind his ear.

She liked his hair and battered cowboy boots. They fit him as well as everything else did in this town. He belonged. She didn't.

Too late to turn back now.

With the sun at her back and her heart pounding, she trudged toward him.

ABOUT THE AUTHOR

I'm an Amazon and international bestselling author who writes passionate romance for every taste—heat with heart— for traditional publishers (NY) and indie. Booklist, Publisher's Weekly, Romantic Times and numerous online sites have praised my work. I've won Readers' Choice Awards, was named a finalist in the EPIC competition, received a Book of the Year award, The Golden Nib Award, awards of merit in the RWA Holt Medallion competitions, and second place in the NEC RWA contests. I'm featured in the Novel & Short Story Writer's Market. Before penning romances, I worked at a major Hollywood production company in Story Direction. My romance genres include erotic, erotica, romcom, historical, contemporary, PNR, and suspense.

Website Link (and Social Media Links):

Website/Blog: http://tinadonahuebooks.blogspot.com/
FB Fanpage: https://www.facebook.com/DonahueTina1/
Newsletter: http://tinadonahuebooks.blogspot.com/p/newsletter.html
BookBub: http://bit.ly/2phWWDu
Instagram: https://www.instagram.com/tinadonahuebooks/
Goodreads: http://bit.ly/1wFmIu6
Twitter: https://twitter.com/tinadonahue
Facebook: http://on.fb.me/1Dl8DHy

Triberr: http://bit.ly/1CE2ec7
Pinterest: http://bit.ly/1yFLeMx
TRR: http://bit.ly/1vb7eEc
Sweet 'n Sexy Divas: http://bit.ly/1ChWN3K
Romance Books 4 US: http://bit.ly/1JPtfeS

www.ingramcontent.com/pod-product-compliance
Lightning Source LLC
Chambersburg PA
CBHW070538130626
46555CB00003B/1483